STORIES FROM
AN [illegible] NA

Written by Brian Heaton and Michael West

Illustrated by Clyde Pearson

---

850 word vocabulary

LONGMAN

LONGMAN GROUP LIMITED
London
Associated companies, branches and representatives throughout the world

*First published *1964*
*New impressions *1966 (twice); *1968;*
**1969 (twice); *1970; *1971;*
**1973; *1974;*
**1976; *1977; *1978*

ISBN 0 582 53438 0

The vocabulary of the New Method Supplementary Readers has been slightly enlarged to include words certain to be known to all readers at each stage. Words outside this vocabulary are explained or illustrated in the text and listed at the end of the book.

Printed in Hong Kong by
Sheck Wah Tong Printing Press Ltd

CONTENTS

One

THE WEAVING MAID AND THE COW-HERD

Chen Li took care of cows: he was a *cow-herd*. Although Chen Li was only a poor cow-herd, he had a magic cow. He went everywhere with his cow, for he loved it very much.

One day he set out to look for a wife, letting the cow lead him from place to place. At last the cow took him to a beautiful river. There was a bridge over the river: the bridge was called the Bridge of the Seven Fair *Maidens*. The cow stopped behind some trees several feet away from the river. Chen Li saw seven beautiful girls laughing and playing in the water.

"These are the seven daughters of the Kitchen God," said the magic cow.

Chen Li was afraid when he heard this, because the Kitchen God was a very powerful god.

"Don't be afraid," the cow said. "The Kitchen God lets them live on the earth like real people."

Then Chen Li pointed to the youngest of the maidens.

"That maiden is the most beautiful of all," he said. "Who is she?"

"She is the youngest of the seven daughters,"

said the cow. "She is called the *Weaving Maid*, because she makes the clothes of all the gods."

Chen Li said, "How can I make the Weaving Maid my wife?"

"I will tell you how you may make her your wife," said the cow. "I will tell you a plan."

Chen Li listened carefully. Then he went quietly to the river and stole the clothes of the Weaving Maid.

The poor girl came out of the river and looked for her clothes, but she could not find them. Then she saw Chen Li holding them, and she cried out. Her sisters ran away at the sight of the young cow-herd.

The Weaving Maid went to the young cow-herd and asked for her clothes: "Please give me my clothes. I will cook and wash for you if you will give me back my clothes."

So the Weaving Maid became Chen Li's wife, and cooked and washed for him. Soon she began to love him very much.

Chen Li and the Weaving Maid lived happily together near the river where they first met. Chen Li worked hard in the fields, while the Weaving Maid washed and cooked. Even the magic cow was very happy.

Perhaps they were too happy. The cow-herd let his cows go where they liked. The Weaving Maid no longer remembered about making clothes for the gods. They cared only for each other.

The Queen of *Heaven* lived up in the sky with the other gods.

After three years the Queen of Heaven became very angry, for there was no-one to make her any new clothes. She sent her servants to the earth. She said, "Order the Weaving Maid to go back to her work!"

The poor Weaving Maid wept sadly because she had to leave Chen Li. She said to her father, the Kitchen God, "Please let me live with Chen Li on earth." But the Kitchen God would not listen to her. Even the Queen of Heaven was sad to see such unhappiness.

At last the great Kitchen God said, "Chen Li and the Weaving Maid may meet once a year on the seventh day of the seventh moon. On all the other days of the year they must not meet. But they may see each other across the river where they first met."

So the Weaving Maid crossed the Bridge of Fair Maidens to meet Chen Li on one day in every year.

When Chen Li died, the Kitchen God let him live in heaven with the other gods. But the Queen of Heaven did not wish to have old clothes again. So she drew a line across the sky.

The Weaving Maid and the cow-herd lived on two *stars* in the sky. The Queen of Heaven had a beautiful *pin* in her hair—a hair-pin. She took her hair-pin and drew a line of stars across the sky between the two stars where the Weaving Maid and the cow-herd lived.

Today, this line of stars is called the Milky Way, and there are two small stars on each side of it. The Weaving Maid and the cow-herd can always see each other across the Milky Way, but they can meet only once every year. On the seventh night

of the seventh moon, all the birds in the world fly high up in the sky and make a bridge of birds across the great Milky Way. The Weaving Maid runs over this bridge to meet Chen Li. If there are clouds in the sky on this night, the birds cannot make the bridge. Then the Weaving Maid and the cow-herd weep and their *tears* fall to the earth in the form of rain.

Anyone who sits under an old tree on this night can hear the sound of weeping as the Weaving Maid and Chen Li go back to their stars for another year.

Two

THE SEVEN BROTHERS

An old man had seven sons. He lived with his seven sons at the foot of a high mountain near the sea. The eldest son was called Strong; the second son was called Wind. *Iron* is a very hard metal. The third son was very hard; so he was called the Iron Man. The fourth son was called Cold Hands, and the fifth son was called Long Legs; the sixth son was called Big Feet, and the seventh son was called Wide Mouth.

One day Wide Mouth (the youngest son) saw the old man looking very sad. He said, "Why are you looking sad? What is wrong?"

"You are all becoming so big! It is hard to grow enough food for you," answered his father. "The mountain is on one side of us, and the sea is on the other side; so we have not enough land to grow the food we need and we cannot get more land."

Wide Mouth called his brothers together. He said, "We must make a large piece of land where we can plant corn."

So in one day they moved the mountain into the sea and made a large piece of good land. The ground was not too hard, but not too soft, not too wet, but not too dry.

Then the brothers planted corn and soon found that they had enough food to eat. They lived very happily there.

The *Emperor* of China was the ruler of that country. He heard about the land which the seven brothers had made. People said to him, "It is very good land, not too hard, not too soft, not too wet, not too dry."

"I shall buy that land," said the Emperor. He sent a letter to the old man: "The Emperor will buy your land."

"But I do not want to sell the land," said the old man. "What shall I do?"

"We shall go to the city," said his seven sons. "We shall go to the Emperor and say, 'O Emperor, do not take away our father's land!' "

When they reached the big city, some soldiers met them. They saw the brothers. They said, "We are afraid of those seven big men! Shut the *gates*!"

So they shut the gates of the city against the seven brothers.

"Open the gates!" said Strong. "We have come to talk to the Emperor."

"Open the gates!" he said again. "Open the gates!"

No-one answered him. He became very angry.

He pulled down the heavy gates with one hand and they went into the city.

The seven brothers went into the city and came to the *palace* (the Emperor's house). There was a strong wooden gate outside the palace.

The second brother was named Wind. Wind said, "We have come to talk to the Emperor. Please open the gates."

"Who are you?" said the soldier. "You are only a simple man from the country. The Emperor is a

We have come to talk to the Emperor

great man. He is the greatest of all men. You cannot talk to the Emperor. Go away!"

"Open the gates!" said Wind, "or I shall blow them down!"

"Go away," said the soldier, "or we shall kill you!"

Then Wind blew—and he blew—and he blew down the gates.

Then the seven brothers walked into the Emperor's palace.

The third brother was named Iron Man. He said, "I shall talk to the Emperor."

As soon as Iron Man came before the Emperor, many soldiers drew out their *swords*.

"Cut off his head!" said the Emperor.

But all the swords were useless. When they touched Iron Man, they broke into small pieces.

"My soldiers cannot stop these men from seeing me," said the Emperor. "Their swords are useless. I must think of some other way of stopping them."

The Emperor said to his men, "Make balls of fire."

They made fire-balls.

Then he said, "Go to the top of the palace and roll the fire-balls down the steps on to these men."

The fourth son was named Cold Hands. He saw the fire-balls.

"Do not be afraid," he said to his brothers. Then he went to the bottom of the steps. He caught each fire-ball.

"The fire is too small. I'm still cold," cried Cold Hands.

Then he threw the fire-balls back at the Emperor's soldiers.

The Emperor was now very angry. He ran about the palace giving foolish orders to everyone.

"Throw them into the sea," he called to some of the soldiers.

But the fifth brother, Long Legs, heard what he said. He answered, "There is no need to throw me into the sea, for I shall be glad to go there by myself."

He took two big steps, and walked into the sea. He walked far out into the sea. But the water covered only his feet.

"This sea is not deep enough for me," he cried. Then he began to catch fish and throw them on to the land.

The other brothers waited in the palace. They waited a long time for Long Legs.

"I'll see where he is," said the sixth brother, Big Feet.

With one step, Big Feet reached the sea.

"Why are you wasting time catching fish?" he asked. "We haven't finished yet."

Then Wide Mouth went down to the sea. He called Long Legs and Big Feet.

"We are wasting time!" he said. "How can we talk to the Emperor? It is useless to talk to the Emperor. He will not do what we ask. Or he will say, 'Yes, you may keep your land'; but he will send soldiers and kill our father. He is a bad man."

"What shall we do?" asked the six brothers.

"Wait here and see what I shall do," said Wide Mouth.

Then Wide Mouth drank up the sea. He ran back to the palace. Then he opened his mouth. The water came out and covered the palace and killed the Emperor.

The Emperor's son became Emperor. He said, "My father was a bad man. The Emperor should not take away land from his people. You may keep your land. You are brave men. When there is a war, you must help my soldiers to fight."

Three

THE DRAGON KING'S DAUGHTER

There was once a poor man called Liu Yee. He studied very hard. At last he went to the big city for his examinations, but he did not pass them. As he sadly walked back home, he saw a beautiful girl. The girl was watching her *sheep* on a small hill near the road. When he came nearer, Liu noticed that she was crying.

Liu asked her, "Why are you so sad?"

The beautiful girl was crying

The girl answered, "I am the youngest daughter of the Dragon King of the Lake of Tung Ting. I was married to the Dragon King of the River Ching several years ago. His servants told untrue stories about me, and the king believed them. He beat me and made me look after his sheep."

Then Liu looked more carefully and saw that the sheep were not the same as other sheep.

"Those sheep are not like other sheep," he said. "What are they?"

"They are called rain sheep," answered the girl. "The Dragon King of the River uses these sheep to make rain."

Only dragons are able to cause rain in China; so Liu knew now that the girl really was the daughter of the Dragon King of the Lake.

"Please give this letter to my father," said the girl.

"But how can I find your father?" asked Liu.

"On the north side of the Lake of Tung Ting there is an old tree. If you hit this tree three times, a soldier will come and lead you to my father."

Liu took the letter and set out on his journey again.

When he reached the north side of the Lake of Tung Ting, he looked around and saw the old tree.

He hit the tree three times; then a soldier came.

"Come with me," said the soldier; then he held out his arm. The lake was cut into two parts to form a road. The soldier led Liu down the road.

Liu went down and down. At the bottom of the lake was a beautiful palace. The top of the palace was made of gold, and there were jewels in all the walls. As Liu came nearer, the big doors opened and he found himself in a large hall. At the end of the hall he saw the Dragon King with many servants on both sides of him.

"The Dragon King wants to know why you are here," said one of the servants.

"I have brought a letter from his daughter," answered Liu.

"Give the letter to the king," ordered another servant.

"Can the Dragon King not speak?" asked Liu. He hoped that no-one would think that he was afraid.

"The great Dragon King does not wish to speak to men like you," said the servants. "He speaks only to other kings."

Liu gave the letter to the King and watched him carefully as he read it. He saw the king's face grow sad as he learnt of his daughter's unhappiness.

"Go to the River Ching as quickly as you can," he ordered his soldiers, "and set my daughter free."

Then the Dragon King turned to Liu. He said, "I thank you for bringing this letter. Rest here in the palace before you begin your journey back to your home."

Just at sunset a loud noise awakened Liu. A servant called him to go to the Dragon King.

Liu went into the hall. There he saw the beautiful daughter of the Dragon King. As soon as she saw Liu, she ran up to him and thanked him. She asked her father to give Liu something.

The Dragon King thought for a long time before he spoke.

"You have helped us very much, young man. I shall give you something which is much better than money," he said. "My army has killed the bad

The Dragon King

Dragon King of the River Ching, so now you may marry my daughter."

Liu was very surprised when he heard these words. He did not wish to marry the daughter of any Dragon King. He looked at the girl.

"I shall be very happy to become your wife," she said.

Liu did not stay to hear any more. He turned and ran away.

A few years later Liu married a girl in his own town; but the girl died soon after the marriage. Liu married again: his second wife also died. Liu was very unhappy. He wanted to have a child of his own, but he had none.

At last he married a third time. This time his wife did not die, but lived and gave him a son. Liu loved his wife very much, for she was beautiful and gentle and kind.

One day, when Liu was holding his small son in his arms, his wife spoke to him.

"I am so pleased that I have given you a son and that you are happy now," she said. "I wanted to find a way to pay you back for helping me."

"What do you mean?" said Liu.

She said softly, "Don't you know that I am the daughter of the Dragon King?"

Four

THE FAIRY NUTS

Once upon a time a mother lived with her three children near a forest. The children were called Seng, Tou, and Po Ki. Seng was the eldest child and often looked after her younger sisters.

One day their mother said, "I am going to visit your grandmother; she lives on the other side of the forest. It is a long journey, so I shall not come back until tomorrow morning."

"Take care of your two sisters, Seng," she said before she left. "Stay in the house and don't let anyone come in."

"Bring back something nice for us, mother," cried Tou and Po Ki.

An old *wolf* saw the mother leave the house. When it grew dark, the wolf came to the door of the children's house. He made himself look like their grandmother.

"Who is it?" the children asked.

The wolf answered, "Open the door for your poor old grandmother."

"But our mother has gone to see you," said Seng.

"We missed each other on the way," said the

wolf. "Perhaps she went by another road."

Seng did not really believe the wolf.

"Grandmother, your voice does not sound the same," she said. But the other two children ran and opened the door.

The wolf quickly stepped inside the house and blew out the light so that the children could not see his face.

"Why did you blow out the light, grandmother?" asked Seng, as she pulled up a chair for her grandmother to sit on.

The wolf did not answer. Then he cried out with pain as he sat on his own *tail*.

The three children asked, "What's the matter, grandmother?"

"I have hurt my back, dear children," answered the wolf. "I think I'll sit on this basket."

The wolf then sat on the basket near the chair and let his tail fall down inside the basket.

"What was that noise?" asked Seng, as the wolf's tail hit the bottom of the basket.

"That is the hen which I have brought for your mother."

Seng did not believe that this was her grandmother. She was afraid. Soon she thought of a plan.

"Do you like nuts, grandmother?" she said to the wolf.

"What nuts?" asked the wolf.

"Fairy nuts, of course," said Seng. "They're so good to eat. If you eat one of these nuts, you will become a fairy and live for ever."

"Are they better to eat than small children?" asked the wolf.

"They grow on a tree near our house. We will climb the tree and bring you some of the fairy nuts."

When they were outside the house, Seng said to her two sisters, "It is not our grandmother! This is a wolf who has made himself look like our grandmother."

"What shall we do now?" they cried.

"I will tell you my plan," said Seng.

They all quickly climbed to the top of the nearest tree and sat there.

Back at the little house, the wolf waited and waited; but still the children did not come. At last, the wolf went to look for them.

"We're up here, grandmother," cried Seng. "These nuts are so good!"

"Bring some down for me," ordered the wolf.

Seng said, "These are fairy nuts and they change when they leave the tree. You must come up here if you want to eat them."

The poor wolf walked round and round the tree, not knowing what to do.

"I cannot climb the tree. Come down at once."

"Wait, grandmother, I have an idea," Seng called out. "Go to the house and bring a long piece of *rope* and a big basket. Then we can pull you up to the top of the tree."

The wolf ran back to the house and soon came back with the rope and the basket. The wolf threw the rope high into the air so that the children could catch it. Then he put the rope round the basket, and got into the basket. "Pull the other end of the rope," said the wolf.

Seng pulled and pulled. When the basket left the ground, Seng let the rope go. The wolf fell down and hit the ground very hard.

"I'm not very strong, grandmother. Are you all right?"

The bad wolf fell to the ground

The wolf's head felt very painful but he still thought only of the fairy nuts.

"Foolish girl," he cried. "Ask one of your sisters to help you to pull the rope."

So Seng and Tou pulled together, and the basket went up more quickly. It was much higher up: then it suddenly fell down to the ground a second time.

"The rope fell through our fingers, grandmother. Are you badly hurt?"

The wolf hit the ground harder this time and broke one of his legs. But he still wished to reach the nuts.

"All three of you must pull me up," he called in a strong voice. His voice sounded more like a wolf's voice than an old woman's.

"Yes, I shall help, too," cried Po Ki. "When you reach the top, the nuts will make you well again."

The wolf called angrily, "Be very careful. If the basket falls again, I shall eat you all."

The children began to pull, and the basket rose higher and higher until it was almost at the top. The wolf was just opening his mouth for the nuts; then the children dropped the rope. The bad wolf fell to the ground like a stone and was killed.

Their mother came home the next morning. Seng told her about the wolf's visit. They all laughed when Seng spoke about the fairy nuts.

Five

THE TURTLE WITH THE WHITE MARK

Ah Fang was a poor fisherman, but he was very kind. One day he caught a large *turtle* with a big white mark on its head. The turtle looked so sad that Fang did not wish to eat it. He put it gently on the grass near the river and sadly watched it. Its body moved from side to side as it began to walk away.

Several years later Fang was walking on a narrow road up a hill, and he met a rich man with many servants. The rich man was so fat that his body moved from side to side like a turtle's body when he walked.

"Out of my way!" cried the rich man.

Fang was angry when he heard the man's unkind words and would not move. Then the rich man gave an order to his servants: "Pull the man out of the way!"

"There are six of you," cried the young man; "but I shall make you remember the name of Fang!"

As soon as the rich man heard Fang's name, he ordered his servants to stop.

"So you are Fang?" he said in a kinder voice. "I wish to thank you for all you have done. Come with me to my house and eat with me."

Fang was too surprised to speak. He let the man take him up the hill to a beautiful palace. They sat down to a big meal.

"I am the Prince of the River Tau," said the rich man. "I must give you much more than food. I owe very much to you."

While he was speaking, the prince hit Fang on his right arm. When Fang left the palace, he noticed that on his right arm there was a small picture of a turtle with a white mark on its head.

As he walked along, Fang saw a small jewel a few feet below the ground. He made a hole and pulled out the jewel.

When he reached home with the jewel, he saw some money under the floor of his little house. After pulling up a few stones, he found a lot of money.

Next he took the jewel and the money to the owner of a big house near the river.

Fang bought the big house. When he went to live in the big house, he saw some silver hidden under the kitchen floor. The silver made Fang a very rich man.

One day when Fang was walking in his garden, he saw a beautiful looking-glass twenty feet under the ground. He worked hard all day to make a deep hole. Just before night came, he brought up the looking-glass. It was old, but it was very beautiful. Fang carried it carefully back to his house and put it on a wooden table near his bed. Of all the fine things which he had, he liked this looking-glass best. He used to clean it every night before he went to bed.

One day a friend said to Fang, "A beautiful princess is going for a ride in the hills near your house."

Fang had heard much about the great beauty of the princess: he wanted to see her. He took his looking-glass and set out. He hid behind a large rock near the road which the princess would take.

Soon the princess and many fine ladies passed by. They stopped for a short time near the rock where the young man was hiding. Fang stayed behind the rock. He held out his looking-glass so that he could see the princess in it. Her beauty was so great that he fell in love with her.

When she left the place, he put down the looking-glass and felt very sad. In the evening he looked at the looking-glass; the beautiful face of the princess was still there!

As the days went by, Fang fell deeper and deeper in love with the face in his looking-glass. He often took the looking-glass into his garden and talked to the princess, making himself believe that she was a real person.

A servant saw him holding the looking-glass and heard him speaking to the princess. The servant thought, "Fang is quite mad." He told the story to everyone whom he met.

The Emperor Soo was the father of the beautiful princess. The Emperor heard the story.

He said to his servant, "Who is this man?"

"He is Fang," said the servant.

"Who is Fang? Is he a prince?"

"No," said the servant. "He is not a prince."

"Bring him to me!" said the Emperor.

So the Emperor's servant went to Fang's house and said, "The Emperor wishes to see you. Come with me."

When the Emperor saw Fang he said, "Cut off this man's head tomorrow morning."

Next morning soldiers came and took Fang away to cut off his head. The princess saw him as he was being led away. Just as the picture of the princess stayed in the looking-glass, so Fang's picture stayed in the heart of the princess.

"Please let him live," she cried. "I want to marry him."

"He must die," said her angry father. "I shall never let you marry him."

The beautiful princess began to weep. She said, "I shall not eat until Fang is set free." Her servants brought her food, but she would not eat.

Three days passed and the princess ate nothing. The Emperor Soo could not bear to see his daughter looking so ill. At last he set Fang free, and he said to his daughter, "You may marry this man."

Then Fang went home and took all his treasure from under the floor where it was hidden. When he came back to the palace of the princess, he brought with him a hundred servants and much silver.

The Emperor was so surprised that he could not find words to thank Fang. He was very happy and asked all his friends to come to the marriage.

So Fang and the beautiful princess were married. They took the magic looking-glass to their fine house. Fang put the looking-glass in a safe place where he could see it every day. Even when his princess was old, the looking-glass still showed a picture of her as a beautiful young girl—the same face which was in the looking-glass when Fang first saw her.

Soon after their marriage, a visitor came to see them. Fang tried to remember who the man was. Then the visitor said, "I am the Prince of the River Tau. I have come to take back one of the things which I gave you a long time ago." Then he touched Fang's right arm.

"Now I have paid you and I can go back to my home," he said: and he went away.

Fang looked down at his right arm; but there was no picture on it. He knew then how much the prince had given him. He ran to thank him, but outside the house Fang saw only a large turtle with a white mark on its head. It moved its body from side to side as it walked slowly to the river.

Six

THE WOODEN HORSE

A *carpenter* makes things out of wood: a *blacksmith* makes things out of iron.

One day a carpenter met a blacksmith.

"I can make very useful things," said the carpenter. "I am the best carpenter in the world!"

"I am the best blacksmith in the world," said the blacksmith, "and I can make better things than you can."

"No, you can't," answered the carpenter. "I can make things which are both beautiful and useful."

After talking for a long time, the two men said, "We will ask the king who can make the best things."

The wise king heard both men; then he said, "Go back to your homes and make something, and bring what you have made to me in ten days' time. Then I shall see which thing is better."

After ten days both men came back to the king. The blacksmith brought with him a large fish made of iron.

"It is certainly beautiful, but what is the use of it?" said the king.

"My fish can carry many heavy things from one place to another," answered the blacksmith.

"You are a fool if you think that your fish can swim," laughed the king.

The fish was taken to the river and filled with heavy things; it swam quickly from one side of the river to the other.

"You are a great man," said the king, full of surprise. "I shall make you the Head Man of a street."

Then the king turned to the carpenter.

"Now show me what you have made," he ordered.

The carpenter showed the king a wooden horse. It was very beautiful and had many keys on its body.

"This horse is only a plaything. Children can play with it," said the king.

"It can do much more than the fish which you have just seen," answered the carpenter. "There are six keys on its body. If you turn the first key, the horse will fly. Turn another key and it will fly faster. When the last key has been turned, it will fly faster than any bird. You can easily fly round the world on this horse."

The king's son was passing by; he heard what the carpenter said.

"Please let me try the horse," he said to his father.

"No!" answered the king. "We do not know that the horse can fly."

But the king loved his son so much that he always gave him what he wanted. The young prince asked again and again; at last his father agreed.

"Ride very slowly," called out the king as the prince climbed on to the wooden horse. "Turn only the first key."

The prince waved goodbye and turned the first key. The horse rose into the air and began to fly away. The prince and the horse flew higher and higher. Soon the people on the ground looked like ants. Even the palace and the houses seemed like little playthings.

The prince turned the second key; then he turned the third key, and the fourth key. Soon he turned all the keys and flew through the air faster than any bird. He flew on and on until he began to feel quite tired. Then he saw a big city a long way under him. He turned the keys back one by one and the wooden horse began to stop. When he turned back the first key, the horse landed safely on the ground outside the city. The young prince then went to a house and stayed the night there.

The next morning the young prince went for a

The prince and the horse flew higher and higher

walk round the city. He met many people who were looking up into the sky. He, too, looked up but could see nothing.

"What is there in the sky?" he asked an old man.

"Our emperor has a very beautiful daughter," said the old man. "He loves her so much that he will not let anyone see her. He has built a palace high in the sky for her. Every day he goes to see her."

"But how did he build a palace in such a place?" cried the young prince.

"A god helped him to build the palace, and now only the emperor can go there," the old man answered.

The prince thanked the old man. That night he took out the wooden horse and flew up to the palace.

At first the princess thought that her father was coming. Then she saw the young prince standing in front of her. She thought that he must be a god. She said, "Only a god could reach this palace."

The prince fell in love with her as soon as he saw her. He said, "I am a prince. I came here on a flying horse."

As they talked to each other, the princess also began to fall in love with the young prince.

The prince stayed only a short time, for he did not want the emperor to see him visiting the beautiful princess. Soon after he left, the emperor reached the palace in the sky and saw his daughter looking very happy.

"Someone has visited the palace and seen you," he cried angrily.

On the next day the emperor thought of a plan. He sent four of his best soldiers to stand outside the palace. But the soldiers fell asleep, and the prince came again to see the princess. This time, when the emperor came, he found his daughter looking even happier than she did on the day before.

The emperor was now very angry. On the next morning he sent for his wise men. None of the wise men knew how to catch the princess's visitor.

One of the emperor's servants heard this. He said to the emperor, "Put wet *paint* on all the chairs in the palace of the princess. Then we must find the man who is wearing clothes with the paint on them. This man will be the princess's visitor."

"The servant's plan is a very good one," said the wise men. So the emperor went up to the palace and put wet paint on all the chairs there. Later, the young prince visited the palace. He sat and talked to the princess. When he was flying back to the city, he saw the wet paint on his coat. He took off his coat and threw it away, although it was covered with jewels.

That night a poor old man was walking along a street in the city and he saw the fine coat. He thought, "This coat is a gift from the gods, because I have always lived a good life." He took the coat with the jewels on it, and ran happily home.

On the next day the emperor sent soldiers all over the city to look for the person who was wearing clothes with the paint on them. They saw the paint on the old man's coat and took him straight to the emperor.

"Cut off his head in the city square," said the emperor.

The people of the city saw the old man being taken to the city square. They asked the soldiers, "Why are you taking him to the square?"

"To cut off his head," said the soldiers.

"Why do you want to cut off his head?"

"Because he visited the princess."

The people laughed. "We do not believe that that old man visited the princess," they said.

Soon the story reached the young prince; he went at once to the emperor.

"I am the person who visited your daughter," he said.

"Set the old man free," said the emperor, "and cut off this boy's head."

The soldiers ran to catch the prince, but he jumped on the wooden horse, turned the keys, and flew away.

He flew up and up until he came to the palace.

He ran to the princess and told her everything.

"Come with me to my father's country. He is sure to like you and he will let us live happily together."

The princess climbed on to the wooden horse, and they flew away.

Then she remembered her two jewels in the palace.

"I must go back for them," she told the young prince. "They are two jewels which my mother gave me before she died. I must give the jewels to the father of the man whom I marry."

"It is foolish to go back now," said the prince.

"I cannot go without my jewels," said the princess. "Your father will laugh at me if I have nothing to give to him."

The young prince sadly turned back the keys of the wooden horse and brought it down.

"Take the horse and come back quickly," he called to the princess. "I shall wait here for you."

The emperor was looking everywhere for his daughter in her palace. As soon as he heard the sound of the horse flying through the air, he hid behind the door of the princess's room. When the princess came in to take the jewels, he caught her. Then the emperor took the princess and the wooden horse to his own palace, and he shut them up in dark rooms. Then he ordered his daughter to marry a very rich man from another country.

The rich man was quite old, but he very much wanted to marry the princess. As soon as the emperor told him of his plans for the marriage of his daughter, the rich man set out from his own country, carrying much gold and silver and many jewels to give to the princess.

But what was the young prince doing during all this time? He waited and waited, and still the princess did not come back. He had no food nor water. So he climbed to the top of a hill. He saw many *fruit* trees on the other side. He ran to them, and took some apples off the nearest tree. The apples were very good to eat. When he had eaten, he felt very tired. He lay down under one of the trees and soon fell asleep.

When he awoke, he touched his face and found that he had a long beard. He was very surprised: he did not know what had happened!

Then he wanted to eat again. This time he did not want any more of the apples, for he thought that they were the cause of his beard. He went to another tree: it was a *pear* tree, and he liked its fruit even better than the apples. Then he lay down to sleep again.

When he awoke, his beard was white and he had two large *horns* on his head. He was very unhappy, for he knew that the princess would no longer love him.

At last he fell asleep.

While he was sleeping, he saw an old man. The old man asked him, "Why are you so sad?"

"I have eaten some of the fruit on the trees," answered the young prince, "and now I have a white beard and horns."

The old man said, "Some of the fruit has fallen down under the trees. The hot sun has made it become brown: it has dried the fallen fruit. Eat some of the dry, fallen fruit. Then go away from this place: it is a bad place. Go away quickly."

When he awoke, the prince ate the dried fruit and his beard and horns went away: his face was as it had been before. The young prince then made a big basket and filled it with both fresh fruit and dried fruit.

For seven days and seven nights the prince walked, looking for a road. All this time, he ate only the dried fruit which was in his basket. At last he saw a road. A man with a donkey was walking along it.

"Please tell me where I am," said the prince.

The man told him.

"So," said the prince, "if I go to the east, I shall reach my own country. If I go to the west, I shall reach the country of the beautiful princess . . . . I will go to the west."

After he had gone a short way, some soldiers and a fine *carriage* passed him. An old man was inside the carriage. He put his head out of the window and saw the prince carrying the basket. He thought, "That is a man selling fruit,—a fruit-seller." He ordered his men to stop.

Then he said to his men, "Bring me some of that fruit. I wish to buy it."

"I cannot sell this fruit," said the prince.

"Don't be foolish," said the old man. Then he called out to one of his soldiers, "Buy the fruit and give the man as much money as he wants. If he won't sell the fruit, take some from him."

The young prince heard this: he tried to tell the rich man about the fruit, but he would not listen. Then he asked one of the soldiers, "Who is this rich man? Where is he going?"

"He is going to marry a beautiful princess," said the soldier.

The young prince asked, "What is the name of the princess?" Then he learnt that she was his own beautiful princess. He took out two large fresh apples and two pears, and gave them to the old man. Then the soldiers and carriage moved on again.

The rich man fell asleep after eating the fruit. When he awoke, he found that he had two horns and a long white beard.

He stopped the carriage and ordered his soldiers to bring the fruit-seller. Soon the young prince was standing in front of him.

"But *I* have eaten the fruit, and look at me," said the young prince.

The soldiers and the rich man looked at the young prince and knew that he spoke the truth.

"Did he fall asleep after eating the fruit?" asked the prince.

"Yes," said the soldiers. "He did. He fell asleep after eating the fruit."

"Then that is the reason why he has grown two horns and a long white beard," said the prince. "In this country, you must never sleep just after you have eaten."

When they heard this, the soldiers wanted to go back to their own country, but the old man ordered them to take him to the princess.

"But you are so ugly! How can she agree to marry you now?" cried his soldiers.

Then another soldier thought of a plan.

"Let's put another person in the rich man's place. Then we can take the princess back to our own country and give her to the rich man there."

"Yes," said the rich man. "That is a very good plan. But who will take my place? We need someone who is young and beautiful."

The soldiers all looked at the young prince.

"We can use this boy," said the soldier. "We shall give him some fine clothes and put him in the carriage. Then everyone will think that he is the rich man who has come to marry the princess."

Soon the young prince was sitting happily in the carriage, while the rich man began the journey back to his own country.

When the young prince and the soldiers reached the city, the emperor was very pleased to see such a fine young man with so much gold and silver and so many beautiful jewels to give to his daughter. He sent for the unhappy princess and said, "The marriage will be very soon."

On the day before the marriage, the young prince spoke to the princess for a short time. It was the first time they were together, and she did not know who he was.

"Look at me," he said. "Do you know me?"

"Yes! Yes!" she cried. "You are my prince who came on the wooden horse!"

"There is no need to be afraid. I have thought of a plan to leave here," he said. "After our marriage, ask your father for the wooden horse. Tell him that you will not go without it."

On the next day the two happy young people were married. Soon it was time to leave, and the princess went to her father. She said, "Give me the wooden horse. I shall not go without the wooden horse."

"Why does she want it?" said the emperor. "She is very foolish. I shall not give it to her."

"It's only a child's plaything," said the emperor's friends. So at last he gave it to her.

When they were outside the city, the rich man's soldiers stayed very close to the young prince and his princess.

When they were near the rich man's house, the young prince said to the princess, "Ask the soldiers to give you a bag of money to give to the poor people of the city." The soldiers gave the princess a bag of money. She then threw the money on the ground round the carriage. Soon many people were running round them, trying to get the money; and the soldiers could not stay near the prince and princess.

The young prince quickly helped the princess on to the wooden horse. He turned all the keys. They both flew, up—up—up, faster and faster until the young prince reached his own country.

The king and all the people in the country were very surprised to see the prince again: they thought that he was dead. And they were very surprised to see the beautiful princess who was his wife!

The king was so happy that he gave the carpenter many jewels. The prince and the princess were married once again and lived happily in a fine palace—on the ground.

Seven

THE BLUE PEARL

Hwa Fu is a town in China. The land there is very rich. Everyone has enough to eat and drink in Hwa Fu town.

Few people know the true story about Hwa Fu, for it was not always a happy place. Many years ago a big fire burnt the whole town and killed most of the people who lived there. A few people ran to a place many miles away.

The big fire in Hwa Fu town kept burning day after day and year after year. Those who ran away from the fire built homes in the new place. After a few years, they married and had children. These children grew up and never saw Hwa Fu.

Then one year no rain fell and all the rivers became dry. Soon there was no water to drink. Every day the men and the boys went on long journeys to look for water.

One of the boys was called Yen Kan. He was very brave and very strong, and went a long way each day to get water. After several months, even Yen Kan began to grow tired of these long journeys.

"What shall we eat and drink when winter comes?" he asked his father.

But his father did not answer him.

"Let's leave here and find a better place to live," said Yen Kan.

"Hwa Fu is the best place to live."

"But Hwa Fu is still burning. Even the stones are on fire. How can we hope to live there?"

Then Yen Kan's father told his son about an old man who visited them a few years after the fire.

"There is a big blue *pearl* in a lake many miles away," said the old man. "That pearl can put out the fire. But there is a giant *spider* there: the spider kills all who come there. There is also a golden queen bee: she lives on the Flower Mountain in the north. She can kill the spider."

"I shall go and get the pearl," said Yen Kan. "Then we can put out the fire at Hwa Fu."

"Do not go!" said Yen Kan's father. "Two men set out to get the pearl soon after the old man's visit, but they never came back."

"We shall certainly die if we do not get any more food or water," said Yen Kan. "What can I lose by trying to find the pearl?"

So the brave Yen Kan set out on his journey to the Flower Mountain. He took with him a bowl for food and water. He walked on and on for many days, eating fruit from the trees and drinking water from the small rivers.

At last he reached a high mountain. He thought that it was the Flower Mountain, so he started to climb up it. He climbed for three days and nights without stopping. When at last he came to the top, he saw hundreds of flowers all around and knew that it really was the Flower Mountain. Many bees were flying round the flowers.

"But how can I see which is the queen bee?" said Yen Kan, "and how can I catch her?"

Yen Kan said, "I have a plan. I shall build a fire. The *smoke* of the fire will drive all the other bees away." He looked for some wood to make the fire, but he could see only one small tree.

While he was still trying to find some wood, a big, ugly bird flew above his head. The big bird was carrying a little bird in its mouth. The small bird was crying with fear, and a beautiful bird was flying behind, trying to save the little bird.

When Yen Kan saw what was happening, he threw a stone at the big bird: it opened its mouth to cry out in pain, and the little bird was able to fly away.

The beautiful bird gave happy cries when it saw that the little bird was free.

The bird said, "Thank you for saving my young one."

Yen Kan was surprised to hear the bird speaking, but he did not answer. He was thinking about the wood for the fire.

"What is the matter?" asked the beautiful bird. "If I can help you, please tell me."

"I am looking for pieces of wood to build a fire," said Yen Kan.

"I can get you as much wood as you need," said the beautiful bird. It flew up very high in the sky and called the other birds.

Soon many other beautiful birds began to fly towards Yen Kan. Each of them carried a little bit of wood in its mouth and dropped it in front of Yen Kan. After a short time there was enough wood to build a big fire.

Soon the smoke from the fire was driving all the bees away. It drove away all the other bees—but not the queen bee. The queen bee stayed.

Yen Kan took off his hat. He said, "I will throw down my hat on the queen bee when she comes out."

He waited—and waited.

Then the queen bee came out from a big flower behind him and flew up in the air, so that Yen Kan could not catch her.

He was about to begin his journey home. Then he saw the beautiful bird flying towards him. She was holding the queen bee. She put the bee in his hand.

The queen bee flew straight at the spider

He took out a little box and put the queen bee in it, and went on his journey to the lake.

At last Yen Kan reached the lake.

As he stood there, he saw the spider. It came out of a hole in the ground. It was the biggest spider he had ever seen. It had long hairy legs and its eyes were like fire.

It looked at him and opened its mouth. It moved towards him.

"If I run away, it will jump on me and catch me," he thought. He stood there. The spider came nearer and nearer.

He took the box out of his pocket. When the spider was very near, he opened the box. The queen bee flew out. She flew straight at the spider—on to its head; and it rolled over, dead.

Yen Kan jumped into the lake. He went down—down—down in the water until he came to the bottom. And there he saw a blue light, and in the middle of the light he saw the pearl.

He took the pearl in his hand: it was very cold. He came up out of the lake and put the blue pearl in his water-pot. The water in the pot was frozen: it became ice.

He travelled back till he came to a hill near Hwa Fu. He looked down at the town and saw fire and smoke. Then he threw the water-pot down into the fire. The fire went out. Heavy rain fell.

So Yen Kan and his father and all the people went back to the town. They built houses there, and were very happy. And some called the town Yen Kan because Yen Kan had put out the fire and saved their town.

Eight

THE TWO SNAKES

Once there were two *snakes;* they were magic snakes. One was a white snake: it was eighteen hundred years old; the other snake was a green

snake: it was only eight hundred years old. They were given the power of changing into two women when they wished to do so.

After a short time, the two snakes quarrelled and began fighting. The battle went on for a whole day. At the end of the day the white snake was the winner: the green snake had lost the fight.

The green snake said to the white snake, "From now on, I shall be your servant."

The Ching Ming *holiday* is a day on which no-one does any work. On this day all the people visit the *graves* of the dead—the places in which dead people are put. They go to clean the graves and to leave food there.

Hsu San was a young man. On this day, Ching Ming, he went with many others up a hill near the West Lake in Hangchow. He went to visit the graves. As he was coming back, it started to rain heavily. He saw an old tree near the bottom of the hill, and ran to it. When he reached the tree, he saw a beautiful lady and her servant standing there. They, too, were trying to keep out of the rain.

Hsu San had never seen anyone so beautiful as the lady. While the rain fell, the young man began to talk to her.

"My name is Hsu," he said. "Please tell me your name."

"My name is Bai Su Ching," said the beautiful lady.

They talked together for some time. Then Hsu said, "Will you have tea with me tomorrow?"

"Thank you," said the lady. "You are a nice young man. I shall have tea with you tomorrow."

Hsu and Bai Su Ching fell deeply in love with each other. Later they were married, and they had a son.

One year during the Dragon Boat holiday, Bai Su Ching drank too much *wine*. When she fell asleep on her bed, she changed back into a snake.

Hsu came into the room. He saw a long white snake on his wife's bed! "Oh!" he cried and he ran out of the house. The servant wakened Bai Su Ching.

"Now Hsu has learnt the truth," she cried. "We must kill him."

But Bai Su Ching did not wish to kill Hsu.

"No! No!" she said. "We must not hurt him. This is what you must do: run into the fields and look for a white snake. When you have found one, kill it and bring it to me."

The servant did as Bai Su Ching ordered. She brought a white snake and put it on the bed. Then Bai Su Ching called Hsu and pointed to the snake on the bed.

"Look at the snake which we have just killed," she said.

When Hsu saw the dead snake, he said, "You are very brave!" And he did not think any more about it.

Some time later Hsu went to the top of the hill early one morning to visit the Golden Hill *Temple*. After praying, he met an old *priest*: the old priest told him about Bai Su Ching and her servant. He told Hsu the whole story about the two snakes: "Your wife was really the white snake," said the priest.

"My wife was the white snake? I cannot believe it!" cried Hsu. "But, if you say so, it must be true." He wept.

"What can I do?" he cried.

"Do not be afraid," said the old priest. "Stay here with me and you will be safe."

When Hsu did not come back home, Bai Su Ching set out to look for him. Soon she heard about the old priest and became very angry. She called her *cousins*, the magic dragons. She said to them, "Send rain down upon the land!"

The sky grew very dark and heavy rain fell for

Hsu and his son saw a white snake rise in the sky

several days, covering all the fields and houses. Each day the water rose higher and higher, but it could not reach the top of the hill where the Golden Hill Temple stood.

The old priest now became angry. He saw what Bai Su Ching was trying to do. So he used a magic pot to catch the two snakes. He caught the green snake and sent it to a cave far away and shut it in.

Then he caught the white snake and shut it in a *pagoda* near the West Lake.

Many years passed. Then, one day a young man visited the Golden Hill Temple. The man had a very sad face. He asked to see his father: "He became a priest in this temple," he said.

"What was your father's name?" asked the priest.

"His name was Hsu San," answered the young man.

"My son!" cried the priest. "I am Hsu San. I am your father."

"Where is my mother?" said the young man. "Can I see her?"

Hsu wept.

"She is not here," he said. "She is in a pagoda near the West Lake. I will show you the place."

Hsu took his son to the pagoda and showed him the place where the white snake was.

The sad young man put food and paper money near the place.

He prayed for his mother. Then he turned to go away. There was a loud noise in the sky and rain began to fall. Hsu and his son saw a white snake rise up into the clouds high in the sky.

They knew that their prayers had set Bai Su Ching free.

Nine

THE PEACOCK PRINCESS

Many years ago there lived a prince named Chowsuton. He lived in a country called Monbanja. Everyone loved him because he was brave and strong and kind.

One night, when he was asleep, he had a *dream*. In his dream he saw a beautiful peacock. Then the peacock changed into a beautiful woman. She was

the most beautiful woman he had ever seen. "She is the most beautiful woman in the world," said the prince. He awoke: then he said to his father, "In a dream I saw the most beautiful woman in the world. I saw the Peacock Princess."

"The Peacock Princess?" said the king. "How can a peacock be a princess? It was only a dream. Dreams are foolish things."

Many beautiful princesses wanted to marry Chowsuton; but he said, "I shall marry the Peacock Princess. I shall never marry any other woman. I shall travel over the whole world until I find her."

So Prince Chowsuton set out. He travelled over mountains and through forests and he asked many people, "Where can I find the Peacock Princess?" But the people laughed. "A peacock is a bird, and a princess is a woman. How can there be a Peacock Princess?"

"Cannot anyone tell me where to find the Peacock Princess?" said Chowsuton.

But the people laughed at him.

At last he came to a little town near a great forest. He saw a very old woman sitting by the side of the road. He asked her, "Where can I find the Peacock Princess?"

She said, "I do not know, but you should ask Lao-Ren. He lives in a cave in the forest; he knows everything."

So Chowsuton went into the forest. He went deeper and deeper into the forest. At last he came to a hill in the middle of the forest. There was a cave in the hill. He called, "Lao-Ren! Lao-Ren!"

An old man came out of the cave. "What do you want?"

"I want to find the Peacock Princess," said Chowsuton.

"Which Peacock Princess?" said Lao-Ren. "There are seven Peacock Princesses."

Then Chowsuton told him about his dream. "I am a prince of Monbanja, and I shall never marry anyone except one of the Peacock Princesses."

"Come with me," said Lao-Ren. "They come to the Blue Lake every seventh day. I will show you the place."

Lao-Ren led Chowsuton to a lake. The water of the lake was as blue as the sky.

"Every seven days," said the old man, "seven princesses come to this lake. They look like peacocks, but they are princesses. They take off their peacock dresses and wash themselves and play in the water. The youngest of them is the most beautiful. Her name is Nannona.

The old man and the prince hid among the trees. "This is the seventh day," said Lao-Ren: "they will come very soon."

After a short time Chowsuton heard a sound in

the air. Seven birds flew down. They took off their peacock dresses and sang and played in the water. Chowsuton said, "I saw that princess, the youngest, in my dream. She is the most beautiful woman in the world!"

The princesses came out of the water and put on their dresses.

Prince Chowsuton said, "Oh, Princess Nannona, let me speak with you before you fly away."

"Who are you?" said the Princess.

"I am Prince Chowsuton. Here is Lao-Ren. He knows everything. He knows that I am a good man and will not hurt you."

So Nannona stayed and talked with the prince; and she loved him. She gave him a ring and said, "Look in the jewel of this ring and you will always be able to see me."

Chowsuton said, "Come with me to my country and be my wife. Then I shall always be able to see you."

So Prince Chowsuton and Princess Nannona went to Monbanja.

The King of Monbanja and his Queen loved Nannona, but the Da-Ren was angry. The Da-Ren was the great man who helped the King to rule the country. He did not want the prince to marry Nannona: he wanted the prince to marry his own daughter.

The Da-Ren sent a letter to the King of the country named Tung: it was the nearest country to Monbanja. He said, "The Princess Nannona is the most beautiful woman in the world, but we do not want our Prince Chowsuton to marry her. Come with your army, and I shall help you."

Everything was being made ready for the marriage of Chowsuton and Nannona. But, on the day before the marriage, the King of Tung sent his army to fight against Monbanja.

Prince Chowsuton led the soldiers of Monbanja against the King of Tung's army.

Then the Da-Ren went to the King and said, "Our army has lost the battle and Prince Chowsuton has been killed. The King of Tung will go on fighting until he gets the princess. You must kill the princess: then he will go away.

Nannona said, "If I must die, I wish to die in my peacock dress."

So the King gave Nannona her dress. She put it on.

As soon as she had put on the dress, she was able to fly. She flew away to her own country.

Chowsuton led the army back into the city. He said "Where is the Princess Nannona?"

Then he heard what the Da-Ren had done. He killed the Da-Ren, and he said, "I shall go and find the princess."

The princess flew away to her own country

He went to the lake where he had met her. He asked Lao-Ren, the old man, "Where can I find Nannona? Where is her country?"

Lao-Ren said, "It is very far away. You must travel for many days across a place where there is no water. You must climb the White Mountain whose walls are like glass. You must cross a river which is very hot. The water is much too hot for anyone to swim in it, and there is no bridge. Will you travel through these dangerous places?"

"Yes," said the prince. "I do not wish to live without my princess."

"Take this magic *stick*. It is made of iron. It will point always towards the city of the Peacock Princesses; and it will help you in all dangers."

For many days Chowsuton travelled across the place where there was no water. There was no water and there were no trees, and the sun was as hot as fire. At last he fell down near a big rock. He said, "I cannot go on. I shall die here and never see Nannona again." Then he hit the rock with his magic stick. Water came out from the rock, and he was saved.

He came to the White Mountain. He tried to climb it, but every time he fell back. At last he said, "How can I climb it? The sides are like glass, and there is no place in which I can put my feet." Then he took the magic stick. He hit the side of the mountain with it. At once the mountain opened, and he ran through to the other side.

Then he came to a dark forest. He saw two very big birds at the top of a tall tree. He climbed up the tree and jumped on to a wing of one of the birds. He hid himself there.

The next morning the giant birds flew over the river which was very hot to the city of the Peacock Princesses.

As Chowsuton walked along the street, he saw a woman carrying a pot of water. He said, "Where are you taking that pot of water?"

She said, "I am taking it to the Princess Nannona."

Then he took the ring off his finger and dropped it into the water-pot when the woman was not looking.

The servant carried the water-pot to the palace.

She poured the water over the princess, and the ring fell out of the pot.

Nannona cried, "That is my ring. That is the ring which I gave to Chowsuton. How did it come into your water-pot?"

The servant said, "I met a young man in the street. He asked me, 'Where are you taking that pot of water?' I think that he dropped the ring into my water-pot when I was not looking."

Nannona said, "My prince is not dead! He is alive, and he has come to find me!"

So Chowsuton married Nannona, and Chowsuton became king of the city of the Peacock Princesses. And Chowsuton and Nannona lived happily ever after.

QUESTIONS

I THE WEAVING MAID AND THE COW-HERD

1. Where did the cow take Chen Li?
2. What did Chen Li see?
3. Why was the youngest daughter called the Weaving Maid?

1. What did Chen Li steal?
2. What did the Weaving Maid say to Chen Li? "I will . . . . "
3. What did she become?

1. Where did Chen Li and the Weaving Maid live?
2. Where did Chen Li work?
3. What did the Weaving Maid no longer remember?

1. Who became very angry?
2. Why did the Weaving Maid weep sadly?
3. When could Chen Li and the Weaving Maid meet?

1. What did the Queen of Heaven draw with her hairpin?
2. Where do all the birds go once every year?
3. What happens if there are clouds on this night?
4. Who can hear the sound of weeping?

II THE SEVEN BROTHERS

1. What was the name of the youngest son?
2. Why was it hard to grow enough food for the brothers? Because they were . . . .

1. What must the brothers make?
2. What did they do in one day?
3. What did the Emperor wish to do?

1. What did the soldiers do?
2. What did Strong do when no-one answered him?

1. What did Wind say to the soldiers? "We have come to . . . . "
2. What did he do to the gate?
3. Where did the brothers then go?

1. What was the name of the third brother?
2. What did the Emperor order his soldiers to do?
3. What happened when the soldiers' swords touched the third brother?

1. What did the Emperor tell his men to make?
2. Where did Cold Hands go?
3. What did he say? "The fire . . . . "

1. What foolish order did the Emperor give?
2. How high did the water reach?
3. What did Long Legs begin to do?

1. Where did the other brothers wait for Long Legs?
2. Who reached the sea with one step?

1. What did Wide Mouth do to the sea?
2. What happened when he opened his mouth back at the palace?
3. What did the new Emperor say? "You may . . . ."
4. What must the brothers do for the new Emperor? They must help his . . . .

III THE DRAGON KING'S DAUGHTER

1. What was the girl looking after?
2. What did Liu ask her? "Why . . . . ?"
3. To whom was she married?

1. What kind of sheep was the girl looking after?
2. What did Liu take?
3. Where was the old tree?
4. What must he do to the tree?

1. What happened when Liu hit the tree three times?
2. Where was the beautiful palace?
3. What was made of gold?

1. What did the servants say to Liu? "The great Dragon King . . . ."
2. What did the Dragon King order his soldiers to do? He ordered his soldiers to go to . . . . , and . . . . his . . . .

1. What awakened Liu?
2. Whom did he see in the hall?
3. What did the Dragon King say? "You may . . . ."
4. What did Liu not wish to do?

1. How many times did Liu marry?
2. Whom was Liu holding when his wife spoke to him?
3. Who was his wife?

IV THE FAIRY NUTS

1. What were the three children called?
2. What did Seng often do?
3. Where was their mother going?

1. When did the wolf come to the children's house?
2. Whom did the wolf look like?
3. What did Seng say about the wolf's voice? "Grandmother, your voice . . . ."

1. Why did the wolf blow out the light?
2. Why did the wolf cry out with pain?
3. Where did the wolf then sit?

1. What kind of nuts did Seng talk about?
2. The wolf asked, "Are the nuts . . . . than . . . . ?"
3. Where did these nuts grow?
4. Where did the three children go?

1. What did the wolf do when the children did not come back?
2. What did the wolf order them to do?—" . . . . "
3. Seng said, "The nuts . . . . when they leave the tree."
4. What did Seng tell the wolf to bring?

1. When did Seng let the rope go?
2. What did the wolf tell Seng to do? He told Seng to ask . . . . her . . . . to . . . .

1. Who pulled the rope the second time?
2. What happened when the wolf fell?
3. What did Po Ki say? "When you reach . . . . "

1. What did the three children do when the wolf was opening his mouth for the nuts?
2. What happened to the wolf?
3. When did the mother come back?

V THE TURTLE WITH THE WHITE MARK

1. Why did Fang not wish to eat the turtle? Because it looked . . . .
2. Where did he put it?
3. What did its body do as it walked?
4. How did the rich man's body move?

1. When did the rich man tell his servants to stop?
2. Who was the rich man?
3. Where did he hit Fang?
4. What did Fang notice when he left the palace?

1. Where was the jewel?
2. What did he see under the floor of his little house?
3. What did he find under the kitchen floor of the big house?

1. Where did Fang see the beautiful looking-glass?
2. Where did he put the looking-glass?

1. What did the friend say to Fang? "A beautiful princess will . . . . "
2. Where did Fang hide?
3. What did Fang see in the looking-glass in the evening?

1. What was Fang doing when the servant saw him?
2. Who heard the story?
3. What did the Emperor order his soldiers to do to Fang when he saw him?

1. What did the princess ask her father? "Please . . . . "
2. What could the Emperor Soo not bear to see?
3. What did he say to his daughter?

1. What did Fang do when he went home?
2. What did he bring to the palace?

1. What did Fang and the princess take to their fine house?
2. Who was Fang's visitor?
3. What did he take back?
4. What did Fang see outside his house?

VI THE WOODEN HORSE

1. Who met a blacksmith?
2. What did the blacksmith say? "I can make . . . . "
3. Whom did the two men ask?

1. What did the blacksmith bring?
2. (a) What was it filled with? (b) What did it do?
3. What did the king make the blacksmith?

1. What did the carpenter show the king?
2. How many keys had it?
3. What will happen when the last key has been turned? The carpenter said, 'When the last key . . . . '

1. Who happened to be passing by?
2. What did he say to the king? "Please . . . . "
3. Which key did the king tell him to turn?

1. What did the people look like?
2. How many keys did the prince turn?
3. Where did the horse land?

1. Where did the emperor build a palace?
2. For whom did he build the palace?
3. Who helped the emperor to build the palace?

1. Who did the princess think was coming?
2. How long did the prince stay?
3. Who came later?
4. Why did he think that someone had come to the palace? Because his daughter was looking . . . .

1. What did the soldiers do outside the palace?
2. What did the emperor do the next morning?
3. What did the servant tell the emperor to do?
4. What did the prince see on his coat?
5. What did he then do?

1. What did the old man think? "This coat . . . . "
2. Where did the soldiers take the old man?
3. What did the young prince tell the emperor? "I am . . . . "

1. To which country did the prince and princess begin to go?
2. What did the princess remember?
3. Who would laugh at the princess if she had nothing to give him?

1. Where did the emperor hide?
2. Whom did he order his daughter to marry?

1. What did the young prince see on the other side of the hill?
2. What did he eat?
3. What did he have when he awoke from the first sleep?
4. What fruit made the horns grow?

1. What did the old man tell the prince? "Eat some . . . . "
2. How long did the prince spend looking for a road?
3. What country will the prince reach if he goes to the east?
4. What country will the prince reach if he goes to the west?

1. Who passed the young prince?
2. Who was in the carriage?
3. What did the young prince give to the rich man?

1. What did the rich man find when he awoke?
2. What did the young prince say was the reason for the beard and the horns? ". . . . after you have eaten . "

1. Who took the place of the rich man in the carriage?
2. What did the soldier say? "Then everyone will think . . . . "

1. Why was the emperor very pleased?
2. What did the princess ask her father to give her?
3. What did the emperor's friends say? "It's only . . . . "

1. Why did the rich man's soldiers stay very close to the young prince and his princess?
2. What did the princess do with the money?
3. What did the king give to the carpenter?

VII THE BLUE PEARL

1. What happened many years ago at Hwa Fu?
2. How long did the fire keep burning?

1. What happened one year?
2. Where did the men and the boys go every day?
3. What did Yen Kan ask his father? "What shall we . . . . ?"
4. Why cannot they go to Hwa Fu?

1. Who visited them a few years after the fire?
2. Where was the big blue pearl?
3. What can the pearl do?
4. What can kill the giant spider?

1. Where did Yen Kan go?
2. What did he take with him?
3. What did he see at the top of the mountain?

1. What did Yen Kan look for?
2. What flew above his head?
3. What did Yen Kan do?

1. What did the beautiful bird say to Yen Kan? "Thank you . . . . "
2. What was Yen Kan thinking about?
3. What did all the birds carry?

1. What did the smoke do?
2. Where was the queen bee hiding?
3. Who brought the queen bee to Yen Kan?
4. What did Yen Kan put the bee into?

1. Where did the spider come from?
2. What kind of legs had the spider?
3. The spider's eyes were like . . . . ?
4. The queen bee flew on to . . . . ?

1. Where was the blue pearl?
2. The blue pearl was very . . . .
3. What happened when he put the pearl in the water-pot?
4. What name did some people give to the town?

VIII· THE TWO SNAKES

1. How old was the white snake?
2. What did the green snake say to the white snake? "From now on, ... "

1. When do all the people in China visit the graves of the dead?
2. Where was Hsu San walking?
3. Where did he meet the beautiful lady?
4. What was her name?

1. When did Hsu's wife drink too much wine? During the . . . .
2. What happened when she fell asleep?
3. What did she tell her servant to do? She told her servant to bring a . . . .

1. Where did Hsu go?
2. What did the priest say? "Your wife is . . . . "
3. What did the priest tell Hsu to do? " . . . . and you will be safe."

1. What did the magic dragons do?
2. How did the priest catch the two snakes?
3. Where did he put the white snake?

1. Who visited the temple?
2. Where did Hsu take the young man?
3. What did the two men see?
4. What did they then know?

IX THE PEACOCK PRINCESS

1. What was the name of the prince?
2. What did the prince see in his dream?

1. What did the prince ask many people?
2. What did the people do?

1. Where did Lao-Ren live?
2. How many Peacock Princesses were there?
3. Where did the princesses come?
4. How often did they come to that place?

1. Which princess did Chowsuton see in his dream?
2. What was the name of the princess?

1. What did Nannona give to Chowsuton?
2. What will he be able to see in the jewel?
3. What did Chowsuton ask Nannona to be?

1. Who helped the king to rule?
2. Whom did the Da-Ren want Chowsuton to marry?
3. To whom did the Da-Ren send a letter?
4. What did the Da-Ren tell him to do?

1. Who led the soldiers against the King of Tung?
2. What did the Da-Ren tell the King of Monbanja?
3. The Da-Ren said, "You must . . . ."
4. What did Nannona do when she put on her peacock dress?

1. Lao-Ren said, "You must travel across a place where there is . . . ."
2. What must Chowsuton climb?
3. What did Lao-Ren give to Chowsuton?
4. What was it made of?

1. What happened when Chowsuton hit the rock?
2. What happened when Chowsuton hit the side of the mountain with the magic stick?
3. Who took Chowsuton to the city of the Peacock Princess?

1. What was the woman carrying?
2. Where did Chowsuton drop the ring?
3. What did Chowsuton become?

LIST OF EXTRA WORDS

blacksmith 6

carpenter 6
carriage 6
cow-herd 1

dragon 3
dream 9

emperor 2

fruit 6

gates 2
graves 8

Heaven 1
holiday 8
horns 6

iron 2

maiden 1

nuts 4

pagoda 8
paint 6
palace 2
peacock 9
pear 6
pearl 7
pin A
priest 8

rope 4

sheep 3
smoke 7
snakes 8
spider 7
stars 1
stick 9
swords 2

tail 4
tears (n) 1
temple 8
turtle 5

weaving
wine 8
wolf 4